1999

# DAD & ME

## by Peter Catalanotto

A DK INK BOOK
DK PUBLISHING, INC.

Today the first American is going to walk in space.

Dad smiles at me and shakes his head. He says we can't listen to the space walk together. This afternoon he has an important meeting. But later we'll watch the evening news and hear all about it.

I love astronauts. I even met one once. He shook my hand, and Mom took a picture of us. Someday I'm going to walk in space. Dad gave me walkie-talkies so I can practice. I like it when he flies my spaceship and radios me while I explore the universe. But now he has a lot of work at his office. Mom's busy with my new baby brother, the alien, so King drives the rocket. King's okay. He's pretty smart. He can shake hands and fetch a newspaper, but he can't talk.

I ride my bike on the driveway until the bus comes. I bump and bounce all the way to school. At ten o'clock the whole first grade goes to the Large Group Room to watch the liftoff. We all join the countdown: "Five, four, three, two, one." Then we scream, "Blastoff!"

I run to tell him about the blastoff
and the picture in the newspaper and my
lifeline disconnecting, but he just growls,
"Move your bike. Now!"

A million stars burst in my body. Hot and cold.

Maybe Dad doesn't care about spacewalking.

When I show him I'm floating all over the universe, he says, "Not now, Tommy."

Dad doesn't care about me.

At supper, Dad reminds me, "No hats at the table."
I tell him it's my helmet, which I need because my lifeline
disconnected and I might float away forever and ever, and . . .
Dad beeps, "No helmets at the table."
It's not fair! I slam my helmet down. Milk flies everywhere.
"To your room," Dad says. "Now!"

I'll show him. I'll float far, far away. I'll hide behind Mars so whenever he looks for me I'll be gone and he'll be sorry.

I take my scissors, paste, and
crayons out of my schoolbag.
   I'll show him. I'll stay in space for
years. The whole world will be
looking for me.

Dad beeps. "Tommy! Where's today's paper?
King?" he yells. "Fetch!"
OH, NO! I try to grab the newspaper, but I can't.

I chase King, but it's too late. Dad has the paper, and he's looking right at me.

I run back to my room.

Dad's right behind me.

I dive under my covers. My body's a fist.
I wait. Eyes closed tight.

I wait. And wait.

Nothing.

Then the walkie-talkie crackles: "Hello?...
Come in, Tommy. This is the Gemini Four rescue capsule....
I got your message loud and clear.... Everything's A-OK....
Hop aboard.... Let's go home."

I squeeze Dad's hand.
He kisses my head.
I say, "Can I drive?"

For Jake, a lucky boy to have such a wonderful dad.

Thanks to George Ella for her thought, Dick for loving
that Vuillard ear as much as I do, my nephew Josh,
and, of course, my dad.

*A Richard Jackson Book*

DK Publishing, Inc.
95 Madison Avenue
New York, New York 10016

Visit us on the World Wide Web at http://www.dk.com

Text and illustrations copyright © 1999 by Peter Catalanotto

Library of Congress Cataloging-in-Publication Data
Catalanotto, Peter.
Dad and me / by Peter Catalanotto. — 1st ed.
p.  cm.
Summary: Tommy is eager to listen with his father to the first American spacewalk, but his father has
to go to work, and when he comes home in the evening they have some trouble reconnecting.
ISBN: 0-7894-2584-X
I. Title.
PZ7.C26878 Dad   1999   [E]—dc21   99-11504   CIP   AC

Book design by Annemarie Redmond

The illustrations for this book were painted in watercolor.

The text of this book is set in 16 point Century Old Style.

Printed and bound in U.S.A.

First Edition, 1999

2 4 6 8 10 9 7 5 3 1